Eliza Andrews

The Brothers; a Novel, for Children

Addressed to Every Good Mother, and Humbly Dedicated to the Queen

Eliza Andrews

The Brothers; a Novel, for Children
Addressed to Every Good Mother, and Humbly Dedicated to the Queen

ISBN/EAN: 9783337002565

Printed in Europe, USA, Canada, Australia, Japan

Cover: Foto ©Andreas Hilbeck / pixelio.de

More available books at **www.hansebooks.com**

THE
BROTHERS;

A NOVEL,

FOR

CHILDREN.

ADDRESSED TO

EVERY GOOD MOTHER,

AND HUMBLY DEDICATED TO

THE QUEEN.

From well-known tales such fictions would I raise,
As all might hope to imitate with ease.

FRANCIS.

HENLEY:

Printed and Sold by G. NORTON;

Sold also by Hookham and Carpenter, New Bond-
street; Owen, Piccadilly; Irking, Curzon-street,
-May Fair; Champante and Whitrow, Jury street;
and Cheyne, Sweeting's Alley, Cornhill, London.
1794.

To *the* QUEEN.

I Prefume to addrefs this diminutive work to your Majefty, from my belief of your being a good mother ; and though I bear all poffible refpect and loyalty to your character as my Queen, I ftill more honour and efteem you for thofe private and domeftic virtues, which will enfure you a crown incorruptible of never-fading glory. With fervent prayers for your happinefs,

I am your Majefty's dutiful Subject,

THE AUTHOR.

Address to Parents.

IT is to be prefumed, no attentive parents will put a book into the hands of their children, till they have judged of its fitnefs, by firft reviewing it themfelves. I fhall, I truft, engage their notice for a moment, and they will not perhaps defpife advice, though offered by the weak efforts of a feeble pen. We will not beftow a thought upon the idle, the diffipated, the unfeeling, carelefs mother—from fuch we turn difgufted! But, ye refpected, pious, fond, and anxious parents; ye whofe hearts are burfting for your children's welfare, ye will confent to be exhorted

horted not to deter, beyond the first and early dawn of reason, the business of instruction and improvement. It is less difficult to prevent ill habits than to conquer them after they have established their dominion. Neglect not then for a moment to fix in the infant breast, that sure and strong foundation of every solid virtue, EARLY PIETY ; *so shall you see your sons grow up as the young plants, and your daughters as the polished corners of the temple.*

If in the following facts one useful hint can be found, my purpose is fully answered, and my trouble amply recompensed ;

" For from the most minute and mean,
" A virtuous mind will morals glean."

THE

THE

BROTHERS, &c.

Women, says St. Paul, enfure their falvation by
the care they take to educate their Children.

IN one of the weſtern counties
of England lived Mr. Sinclair,
where his family had long poſſeſ-
ſed conſiderable eſtates. He had
been ſome time united to an amiable woman, without having been

bleſſ

left with children, and determined, therefore, to educate as his heir the youngest son of his sister, who was married to a gentleman of large property, in the same county, of the name of Clairville. Besides Mr. Sinclair's wish for an adopted heir, he hoped to save, at least, one of his nephews, from the neglect he foresaw would take place in their education at home. Mrs. Clairville was too fine a lady, and too much taken up with herself and fashionable amusements, to spare any time upon her children ; and Mr. Clairville had money for every expence but

their

their education. George and
Harry Clairville were both hand-
fome, well formed boys, though
as different in perfon, as in manners; George, the eldeft, was by
all his Mamma's vifitors, moft taken notice of, as a *fine boy,* which
is the ufual compliment paid to
fize in children; and, if indeed
worth is to be eftimated by the
quantity of flefh, George Clairville without doubt, merited the
praife, as he was very fat and large
for his age, with a round ruddy
countenance, and bold addrefs.
Harry, his brother, on the con-
trary, was pale, thin, and delicate,

pofleffing

possessing that shyness which ever
accompanies true merit. He often escaped notice, or if spoken
to at all, it was by the humiliating
appellation of poor fellow; so
absurd, and unjust, is the indis-
criminate praise of common ob-
servers. Mr. Sinclair easily pre-
vailed upon his sister to resign
Harry, at an early age, entirely
to his care; and from that period
dedicated the principal part of
his thoughts and time to the performance of the duty he had im-
posed upon himself—the proper
education of his nephew; and
his intentions were fully assisted
by

by this lady. Both Mr. and Mrs. Sinclair had themselves a proper sense of religion, and were, therefore, well qualified to instil the best principles into their adopted child; to instruct and improve him became their chief delight; and to do Harry justice, it must be acknowledged, he was eager for instruction. He was naturally good tempered and sensible; to cultivate that understanding which nature had given him, was the determined purpose of his kind relations. They were from the benevolence of their temper, extremely indulgent to

their

their charge ; but it was not that weak misguided indulgence that deforms a human creature into a brute. A boy unfitly humoured or neglected, becomes a bear, who runs wild about your house, to the torment of others, and the ruin of himself.

Mr. and Mrs. Sinclair, in their own habits, held forth a bright example of proper conduct to their pupil ; they accustomed him to early hours, and plain food; they were, however, social and cheerful, and promoted at all times elegant amusements; but, as they were highly polished in

In their manners, they were nice
in the choice of their company,
and they never fuffered their a-
mufements to interfere with their
attention to the ferious and important duty they had underta-
ken—that of forming the human
mind to the beft purpofes of its
creator;—a duty too lightly con-
fidered by fome parents, and totally neglected by others. Harry
foon difcovered a capacity and
talents which gave the moft flat-
tering hopes that they had only
need of diligent cultivation. The
firft book that was given to Harry, after he had been taught his
letters,

letters, was Mrs. Barbauld's, with which (as foon as he could read it) he was highly pleafed; as indeed, who is not? He daily learnt by heart, one of thofe beautiful hymns, written by Dr. Watts, of pious memory; he repeated numberlefs things in an emphatic ftile, particularly an extract from the admirable fermons of Dr. Blair, which I cannot help giving my readers, in hopes they will feel the force of it as Harry did, and act according to its dictates.   Truth cannot be expreffed in better or ftronger language,

" Let

" Let not the feafon of youth
" be barren of improvement, fo
" effential to your felicity and
" honour. Your character is
" now of your own forming;
" your fate is, in fome meafure,
" put into your own hands.
" Your nature is as yet pliant
" and foft. Habits have not ef-
" tablifhed their dominion; pre-
" judices have not pre-occupied
" your underftanding; the world
" has not had time to contract
" and debafe your affections;
" all your powers are more vi-
" gorous, difembarraffed, and
" free, than they will be at any
                              " future

B 3

" future period. Whatever im-
" pulfe you now give to your
" defires and paffions, the direc-
" tion is likely to continue ; it
" will form the channel in which
" your life is to run ; nay, it
" may determine an everlafting
" iffue. Confider then the em-
" ployment of this important
" period, as the higheft truft
" which fhall ever be committed
" to you, as in a great meafure
" decifive of your happinefs, in
" time and in eternity. As in
" the fucceffion of the feafons,
" each, by the invariable laws of
" nature, affects the productions
"of

" of what is next in course; so,
" in human life, every period of
" our age, according as it is well
" or ill spent, influences the
" happiness of that which is to
" follow. Virtuous youth gra-
" dually brings forward accom-
" plished and flourishing man-
" hood; and such manhood paf-
" fes of itself, without uneasiness,
" into respectable and tranquil
" old age. But when nature is
" turned out of its regular
" course, disorder takes place in
" the moral, just as in the vege-
" table world. If the spring puts
" forth no blossoms, in the sum-

" mer

" mer there will be no beauty,
" and in autumn no fruit: so, if
" youth be trifled away without
" improvement, manhood will be
" contemptible, and old age mi-
" serable."

Harry was soon perfect mafter of his Catechifm, and was never fuffered to go to bed or to
breakfaft, without having firft
faid his prayers. He very foon
learnt that God alone could protect him from the perils of the
night, or guide him with his
grace, through the duties of the
day; thus, in his infant mind,
was laid that foundation EARLY
PIETY.

PIETY, from which rock there is no falling. Due attention was also paid to his health and growth; at proper times, after his studies, he daily mounted his horse, and rode upon the lawn before the house, till the bell rang for dinner. A description of his favourite steed, may not be disagreeable to my readers; he was of no common mould; he possessed none of the vices or diseases incident to that race of animals; he scorned the gross qualities that belong to flesh and blood; he was slim, and delicately constructed; but, beyond

B   a doubt,

a doubt, the safest nag a man of
Harry's age could ride ; his body
being cane, and his head gold,
with a bridle of filk ; for, to confefs the truth, this much admired
nag of our hero's, was no other
than his uncle's walking ftick,
which Harry daily mounted, with
as much glee and pride, and with
a great deal more fafety and pru-
dence, than the wife heroes of
the turf do their prancing fteeds
of exalted pedigree. Nor could
any of their grooms be more at-
tached to, or more careful of their
courfers than Harry Clairville
was of his fteady Palfrey : after
it

it had carried him safely, (and it never fell with him, for he was too good and too merciful to ride hard) it was his conſtant practice to put it up in what he called its ſtable; namely, a ſnug corner in his uncle's library. He never was careleſs in any thing, nor did he leave it out, as ſome boys would have done, to ſtray, or what was more likely, to be ſtolen. In bad or wet weather, he found amuſement in a little ſtudy, which had been fitted up for him, by his own directions, and furniſhed according to his own taſte. Beſides well choſen books, it contained dissected maps of every description, historical and religious. He had, in his apartment, also, recesses for every sort of study, for sport or exercise; tops, marbles, balls, bats, &c. though he was not fond of cricket, a little friend of his having received a blow on his eye, with a cricket ball; for the same reason, he was careful not to use his bow and arrow, except to shoot at a target when any of his companions were with him, (and he had a great many visitors, for every body loved his company) left any of them should be hurt. It

must

must not be imagined from this, that Harry was too timid; he was only fearful where he could hurt or offend : Where he could protect or defend, he was brave, manly, and spirited to the highest degree, beyond his years. That he had a benevolent, generous disposition, was very soon discovered, whilst he was yet very young: He surprised Mrs. Clairville, one morning, as she was sitting at her dressing room window, by running across the lawn, naked, except his shirt: She flew to meet him, supposing some thief had got into the gar-

den,

den, and robbed him of his cloaths; before she could express her agony at such an apprehension, he burst into a fit of laughing at himself, saying, "How odd I look! don't I look very comical?" "Odd, indeed, my dear child, what has happened to you?" "Nothing at all, aunt, only poor Tommy Jenkins had got such a dirty, ragged coat on, I would make him take mine; so pray send him my shirt, for you know I would not come in quite naked." Mrs. Clairville's eyes glistened with delight at this transaction, and, as soon as she

had

had taken care to have her nephew dreſt, ſhe, with pleaſure,
obeyed his wiſhes, and diſpatch-
ed her ſervant with a ſhirt to
Tom Jenkins, ſuitable to the
cloaths he now had got poſſeſ-
ſion of by Harry's benevolence.
Tom was not unworthy, as will
appear hereafter, of the favour
ſhewn him; from this event, he
became a favourite in the family.
Harry had ſhewn much judgment, in chooſing this little pea-
ſant, above all others, for the object of his bounty. His parents
were honeſt, induſtrious people,
and had kept their ſon conſtantly

at

at fchool, and made him go regularly to church. Mr. Sinclair
fupported at his own expence, a
Sunday School, and honeft Tom
was the mafter's favourite fcholar, on account of his attention
to his learning, and his obedience at all times, to the advice
that was given him.

Though we quit the houfe of
Sinclair with regret, it is time to
turn our eyes to what George is
doing. We feel no pain in leaving our favourite Harry, who is
purfuing the path that leads to
righteoufnefs, and have no doubt
of finding him much improved
at our return.

CHAP-

CHAPTER II.

As righteousness tendeth to life, so he that pursueth evil pursueth it to his own death.—
Proverbs, chap. xi. ver. 19.

MRS. Clairville, unhappily
for her son, had not herself been
properly educated. She possessed none of those elegant accom-
plishments, those various resour-
ces within herself, that could
make a retired country life plea-

fant, or even supportable to her.
She had no knowledge of music,
no skill in drawing, and very little taste for reading or working.

Mr. Clairville, who had more
sense and information, found in
his wife, from the deficiency in
her attainments, a very uncongenial companion ; therefore, to
avoid the languor of a family
party, in such a case, but too
readily fell into those habits, in
which she delighted to pass her
time, namely, in public places of
amusement, balls, routs, cards,
&c. To obtain these, except a
very few months, when fashion
compelled

compelled them to go to their
country houfe, they lived in London; where the morning (if it
can be called morning) is paffed
in plans of drefs and amufement
for the evening. The important
and delightful tafk, to " rear the
tender thought," to improve and
obferve the opening mind of her
infant fon, was no part of Mrs.
Clairville's employment. He
was placed in the higheft part
of the houfe, left his infantine
fports fhould difturb his mother
or her company ; and if, by any
chance, he was permitted to
make his appearance, he was let
in

in much in the ſtile of a New-
foundland puppy, and generally treated as ſuch ; for he was
very ſoon thought noiſy and
troubleſome, and after he had
rumbled about for ſome time,
got correĉted, howled, and was
then turned out. Thus paſſed,
in total neglect, the firſt ſeven
years of this unhappy boy's life ;
without one kind friend to " pour
the freſh inſtruĉlion o'er the
mind," no tender parent, with
anxious care, to fix the " pious
purpoſe in his ſoul" or guide his
infant ſteps aright. Servants
were his chief, indeed, his only
companions.

companions. Deſtructive aſſo-
ciates! No wonder his expreſ-
ſions were groſs, his ideas mean
and ſordid. As his attendants
were too indolent and too ignorant, or perhaps had no direction
to controul him, he became tur-
bulent, arrogant, and overbear-
ing. From the nurſery he de-
ſcended to the *ſtables*, where
grooms and helpers gave a *finiſh*
to an education ſo *proſperouſly*
begun. He was frequently left
in the country, for fear town
air ſhould injure his health; this,
at leaſt, was the affectionate excuſe his mother found for not
                              being

being troubled or interrupted by
his company; the fervant, whofe
particular bufinefs it was to attend
him, found it convenient to confider him now at an age to take
care of himfelf, and permitted
him to be alone in the pleafure ground, making him however promife he would neither
eat fruit or climb trees; but as
he had never been taught the ne-
ceffity of truth, or the difhonour
of a lie, he made no fcruple to
forfeit his word; and it was his
conftant cuftom to indulge in
both thefe habits as appetite or
fancy led him.—God, however,
who

who abhors a *liar*, feverely pu-
nifhed him for his breach of promife. He one day climbed a
tree for the cruel purpofe of
taking a bird's neft, and as he
was returning with the neft in one
hand, the other flipped from the
branch he held, and down almoft from the top of the tree, he
fell, and fhattered one of his
legs in a miferable manner, both
bones being broken. His fcreams
brought the fervants to his af-
fiftance, who could not pity the
fufferings he had fo defervedly
brought upon himfelf by the for-
feiture of his word. Proper care
was

was taken of him, and an exprefs
fent to fetch his mother, whofe
regret for her fon's misfortune
was greatly encreafed by her
being obliged to give up Rane-
lagh for that evening, and in decency fet off immediately for her
country feat. Mr. Clairville,
though fhocked at the caufe, was
not fo unwilling as his wife to
leave London. They found
George, in a ftate truly diftref-
fing. Not being accuftomed to
any reftraint, he was impatient
and ungovernable; he could
not bear the confinement that
was neceffary to reftore his
limb;

limb; he refufed to take, any medicine, and by his obftinacy greatly encreafed his malady, and in a few days he had a fever that endangered his life. His parents, particularly his father, began now, for the firft time, to reflect upon their conduct, and to reproach themfelves for their neglect of his education; and determined, if God fhould be pleafed to permit him life, they would fend him, as foon as he recovered, to fchool. It was indeed full time, or rather five years too late.

CHAPTER III.

I have taught thee in the way of wifdom, I have led thee in right paths.—Proverbs, chap. iv. ver. 11.

WE have not any affection for this headftrong boy; we will not fet by his bedfide all the time of his confinement, but conduct our readers to the abode of his brother, where upon the fame day that George broke his leg,

there

there was a scene of confusion
and distress from a very different
cause. When the dinner bell
rang, and Mrs. Sinclair expected
Harry to make his appearance,
as usual, at the sound, the servants
came in, pale and agitated, desi—
ring their master and mistress not
to be alarmed, but that they had
searched every place in the
house and garden, and Master
Clairville was no where to be
found. "Not to be found!" ex—
claimed his uncle and aunt, both
in a breath, "How dare you
bring me such cruel intelligence!
fly this instant every one of you,

different

D,

different ways, to feek him. Not
to be found! it cannot, muſt not
be!" Away flew the fervants,
joſtling and tumbling over one
another, to ſhew their readineſs
to obey the agonizing and impatient command of their maſter
and miſtreſs, though, to fay the
truth, they had fearched diligent-
ly and with real anxiety before.
There was not one of them, that
did not doat upon their young
maſter; he was kind and civil to
them, but never familiar, or con-
verfed with them : they therefore
loved and refpected him. After
they had a fecond time examined
the

the house, garden, green-house, hothouse, pleasure ground, shrubbery, &c. in vain, they recollected, that sometimes he strolled into the village; for there were but few houses, and the inhabitants were honest, clean, industrious people, supported chiefly by the bounty of their squire. Harry was frequently, the happy agent of various gifts to them; indeed, when he had any money of his own, his first wish was to carry it to Goody Jenkins, mother to his favourite Tom. To every cottage in the village they ran with anxious speed, and every soul

within

within them (that was not crip-
pled) joined in the fearch, with
heavy hearts and ftreaming eyes.
But who will defcribe the ftate
of mind of his uncle and aunt,
during this interval, or their dif-
traction, when all hope was fled
by the return of this groupe of
fervants and villagers, without
fuccefs. Where could he be?
there was no water near, and if
there had been, Harry, now eight
years old, had too much fenfe
not to know the danger of water; yet ftill, where can he be?
enquired each eagerly of the
other, though each was fure, nei-

ther

ther knew. Oh fad! The dinner remained untouched upon
the table ; Mr. and Mrs. Sinclair
fat penfive and filent, benumbed
with grief. The numerous at—
tendants, who crouded round
to comfort, or to receive further
orders, were not fo dumb in
their forrow: each recounted
fome beauty, or fome virtue, that
their dear, fweet, young mafter
poffeffed ; each remembered
fomething that he had faid or
done. The honeft old coachman recollected how often he
ufed to call out of the coach
window to him not to whip the

poor

poor horſes. "Sweet ſoul! he could not bear any poor beaſt ſhould be hurt.—The butler declared, it was but two o'clock when he paſſed him in the paſſage, and ſaid, as uſual, " How do you do, James ?" for he never was above ſpeaking to any one. The houſekeeper, the worthy Mrs. Steady, when ſhe could articulate, which ſhe hardly could for weeping, ſobbed out, that he could not have been loſt long, for at three o'clock he came to ſee if ſhe had fed his parrot, that hung in her room : She ſhould have been happy, if he had ſtaid and

and eat fome jelly that fhe was making, but, God blefs him, he would never ftop a minute: but now, fhe fhould never fee him again, or know another happy hour.

The difcourfe of thefe good folks, though fincere and well meant, added to the deep forrow of the dear child's affectionate relations; and Mrs. Sinclair had juft raifed her head from her hand to thank them for their kind concern, and to beg them to retire, when fhe perceived little Jenkins, running out of breath, who, finding all the doors open,

E   purfued

pursued his way without ceremony into the dining parlour, where the family were all assembled, screaming out, all the way he came, " Pray come, come directly, and fetch Master Harry down.' In an instant Tom was so surrounded, and had so many questions, from so many lips put to him at the same time, that not knowing who to answer first, he stared, without uttering a word. Mr. Sinclair, at last, suppressed the inquisitive impatient tumult, by commanding silence, and insisting upon a clear answer to the question, " where is our dear child ?'

child?"—Tom who was as anxious to inform him as he was to know, took Mr. Sinclair by the skirt of his coat, and still out of breath, said "If you comes along with I, I'll shew you, for he cannot come, the cannot get down, if you, or some of you, does'nt come to help 'em. You must come over yon copse, and through that there gate, as goes to that there field as goes—"

Mr. Sinclair, finding the description Tom was about to give, would take more time than going to the place itself, if it was ever so far off, ordered him to lead

lead the way, without farther talk, and he and all the servants followed, leaving poor Mrs. Sinclair alone, to wait some time longer in painful expectation.

I will thank my young readers for a simile, and beg they will tell me, for I know not, who was ever so proud as Tom Jenkins, at the moment he set off as leader to this honourable cavalcade of master and men. He flew before them across the fields, up one lane, down another, across the close, through the copse, clearing in his way gates, stiles, hedges, ditches, with so

much

much agility and adroitnets, that
with 'no' fmall difficulty the
proceffion that followed, could
keep up with him. The old
houfekeeper, whofe kind curiofity led her on in the purfuit,
was left puffing and blowing
very far behind: fhe thought it
moft prudent to wait the event
upon a ftile half-way, and join
the proceffion again upon its return. Mr. Sinclair, naturally
not very nimble himfelf, was almoft exhaufted, with the length
of the way and Tom's fpeed,
when happily he difcovered the
dear object of all his hopes and

all

all his cares, seated very compo-
fedly, though not very fafely, at
the top of a large tree. Proper
care, however, was taken, and
proper means ufed to relieve and
bring him down fafe. His
uncle took him in his arms, and
the tears that refufed relief to
his anxiety, joy made to flow
plenteoufly. As foon as he was
able to enquire, it was explained
to him how Harry got into this
perilous and extraordinary fitua-
tion. My readers will, I dare
fay, be glad to be informed, as
well as Mr. Sinclair; you mult
know, then, that Tom had

brought his young master a bird's
nest, though no one who knew
Tom would suspect that he had
taken it, as indeed he had not;
he had given a halfpenny for it
to another boy, and carried it as
a present to Harry, thinking
as he knew him to be fond of
birds, that he would be pleased
with it. Harry, who possessed
a generous warmth of temper, required with impetuous haste, to
be conducted to the boy from
whom the nest was bought; he
was soon found, and commanded
by our hero to conduct him to
the very place he had taken it
from,

from, which was the tree above named. Harry, fearlefs of danger while he followed the impulfe of humanity, climbed up to the top branch with great agility, to the aftonifhment of Tom and half a dozen dirty boys, who had followed with curiofity and wonder at Harry's earneft eagernefs to replace the neft, which they, a little while before, had been as refolute in ftealing; after he had, with the utmoft caution and tendernefs replaced it in the very fpot they direfted, and feated himfelf fecurely on a limb of the tree, he thus addreffed sed himself to the idle plunderers beneath him :—" Oh you cruel unthinking boys! have you never been taught how inhuman an act it is to take a nest of eggs? Have you never been made to observe and consider the con—struction of the nest? (for all this I have been taught) that it is one among the many wonderful works of God, which cannot be imitated by the art of man ; that the poor little parent bird has been building it, with infinite la-bour, for many weeks, and all the reward she hopes for her toil, is bringing to life her little brood,

F   which

which she will, with the same unremitting attention, nourish and protect, in a manner that holds forth a bright example to every human mother; and, can you, in wanton, thoughtlefs fport, deprive an innocent bird of this fweet reward, rob her of every joy, and fend her, a reftlefs, wretched wanderer, reduced to a hopelefs fearch, for her chirping, harmlefs family? and this cruelty you commit from the wanton barbarous cuftom of blowing eggs to ftring them upon your heads, or in your houfes, where they hang as trophies of your ig-
norance

norance and inhumanity." Upon
this inexhauſtible ſubject would
Harry have proceeded in his
compaſſion for the enchanting
warblers ſome time longer, if his
honeſt friend Tom had not interrupted him, which nothing however, but fears for his ſafety,
would have induced him to do ;
for he felt himſelf delighted and
improved, by all he ſaid, but it
alarmed him to ſee his beſt and
kind benefactor in ſo dangerous
a ſituation, and, without any apo-
logy for the liberty he took in
interrupting him in his diſcourſe,
called out, " Sir, do you ſee as
how

how it is a getting almost dark? Do they know at home, where you bes comed? La! how they will look up and down for you, and I would not for all my life, as you should come down without Mr. James, or coachman, or some on'em to see as you gets down safe, and if so be as you should fall, it would be the death on'em at the castle. So (nodding his head, to enforce the strength of his argument,) you stop where you be, and I'll soon fetch 'em to you;" and without waiting for Harry's consent, away he flew with all the zeal

and

and speed we have already de-
scribed, for assistance. The pangs
of Harry's absence were forgotten and forgiven in the joy of
seeing him safe again. Young
Jenkins was highly applauded
for his conduct; the grateful affection he discovered for Harry,
had endeared him to the whole
family. Mr. and Mrs. Sinclair,
now restored to peace and joy,
sat down comfortably to the
meal that had been delayed by
Harry's absence; they viewed
him with delight; tears of sensibility mingled with their smiles,
when they reflected upon the
                              generous

generous purpose that had detained him; the domestics were eager to testify how sincerely they participated in their master's joy, at the dear child's return. The cook entreated the butler to give her leave to carry into the room a little pudding, of which she knew him to be particularly fond; Mrs. Steady, the good old housekeeper, came to the parlour door, with all that decorum and respect for which she was truly eminent, humbly begging permission to present with her own hands, to young master, some India sweetmeats of
her

her own, that had been fent her by a coufin of hers, who was a captain. The butler propofed to his mafter, fetching up a bottle of that old fack, that had been fo long in the cellar, for Harry, for once, to have a glafs of it warmed, as he had fafted fo long. The reft had nothing indeed to offer, but they all peeped in to take a look at his fweet face, and departed with a prayer to God, to blefs him for ever. So certainly do worthy actions merit and meet the praife of all.

CHAP.

CHAPTER IV.

A foolish son is a grief to his father, and
bitterness to her that bare him.—Proverbs,
chap. xvii. ver. 25.

WHILST Harry inspired
every breast with love and ad-
miration, his unhappy brother
created disgust, and was equally
disliked by his attendants and
neighbours. His uncontrouled
temper and boisterous manners

rendered

rendered him troublesome to the one and offensive to the other; they rather rejoiced than grieved at the accident which occasioned his confinement. The lads in the village were overheard to say, "So, Master Clairville is very bad with a broken leg; well, I can't say as I be sorry, he can't set the great dog at us now."—"No," says another, "and what's more, he ban't able to put Jacky Smith's t'other eye out with gunpowder. I never saw such a huge stone in my life as he threw in at neighbour Pope's window; it frighted she deadly,

G   as

as fhe fat a fpinning. Poor boy, as I be, I would not have fuch tricks as he has for all the world! Why, it was but the week before he tumbled out of the tree that he killed poor Dame Winny's cat, as pretty a cat fhe was as need be feen. He'll never come to no good, father fays he wont, he's fure, for his wickednefs and cruelty to poor dumb beafts as can't help themfelves."

.We perfectly agree with thefe lads in their juft cenfure; for true it is that *a righteous man regardeth the life of his beaft.*

Miferable

Miferable George! His attendants thought no better of him than his neighbours; he was to them furly, impatient, and impertinent; from their pernicious counfels many, indeed moft, of his faults arofe; yet they were the firft to defpife him. If a young man has any fpark of proper pride within his breaft, this reflection will preferve him from the fociety of mean perfons, namely, that they are the firft to contemn and defpife thofe whom they have by their bad example and advice corrupted.

His

His parents then were the only persons that felt for George's sufferings, and their feelings were of the strongest nature—self-reproach. They were now conscious of their neglect, and lamented they had not by proper care in his infancy, avoided those ills which were likely to bring evil upon their child, and deep sorrow upon themselves; they perceived, too late, that as the scriptures emphatically express it, *they had built their house upon the sands.*

There are a few instances, where children have had so much natural

natural fenfe, and to whom God has imparted fo large a portion of his grace, that they have taken care and pains to improve themfelves in piety and learning; but, I believe this does not often happen, nor, indeed, can it be fuppofed. Is there a plant in our garden that does not require the foftering aid of culture to affift its growth and produce its beauty? How would the gentle rofe preferve its blooming fweetnefs amidft intrufive and contaminating weeds! Would they not render it in its nature, corrupt and degenerate? How then

shall

ſhall the human mind expand, rude and uncultivated, without an anxious parental guide to bend its courſe aright! Without the inſtruction of the experienced, how will the unſuſpecting youth be able to ſhun the ſtorms and quickſands he will find in bad examples, of which there are too many in the world, ready to draw him into the path of deſtruction ! But if EARLY PIETY be implanted in him, then will he be as the houſe built on a rock, and will ſee evil only to avoid it.

A fine lady, like Mrs. Clairville, taken from the height of
town

town diſſipation, and confined, as common decency required, to her ſon's chamber, without company, and without cards, will, no doubt, find time hang very heavy upon her hands. She determined, therefore, to take off the *ennui* of a family party, by inviting her brother, Mrs. Sinclair, and Harry, to paſs ſome time with her, thinking their ſociety preferable to being alone. The family of Sinclair, were ſomewhat ſurpriſed at the invitation, as Mrs. Clairville had never ſhewn any inclination, till now, for their company, and no wonder, as they

never

never played at cards, and her
brother was too apt to put her in
mind how neceſſary and proper
it was to give up more time to
the care and education of her
ſon than ſuited her inclination;
Mr. Sinclair, however, in the
tenderneſs of his heart, forgot her
faults, whilſt he pitied her for the
misfortune that had befallen
George; and, though at any
other time, he would have refuſed
her invitation, he was now determined to comply with her re-
queſt; he would have objected
ſtrongly to Harry's paſſing any
time with his brother, if he had
been

been in health; but when his temper was foftened by illnefs, he thought there might be fome chance of Harry's being of fervice to him; at leaft, George would be unable to draw him into fcrapes and danger. After a confultation, therefore, with his amiable wife, (for her good fenfe and good conduct had made her worthy to be confulted on all occafions) it was refolved to prepare for a vifit to Clairville Lodge. The firft fine morning was fixed upon to fet out. Mr. and Mrs. Sinclair in a neat travelling chaife, and our hero on horfeback;

horſeback; he had, as may be ſuppoſed, for ſome time, laid a-ſide his gold-headed nag, and now mounted a beautiful long-tailed poney, quite as gentle and ſafe as his cane one.

Picture to yourſelf, my dear readers, Harry Clairville, at the moment of his departure, and you will ſee a youth, elegant in his perſon, neat in his dreſs, with that bloom of health with which regularity of life paints the cheek, with that chearful ſerenity that a pure and uncorrupted heart gives to the countenance: and if you can figure to yourſelves,

ſtrongly,

ſtrongly, the reſemblance of a ſoul replete with every noble virtue, and ſeeing, can admire it, you will, I hope, imitate my hero, and be as amiable as he was.

"God bleſs you, Sir," ſaid the old butler, as he lifted him on his horſe, "I wiſh you a good journey; you will do your brother good, if any body can." The good old Mrs. Steady ſmiled a-croſs the court yard, and placed a baſket in the carriage, with a few refreſhments for her dear young gentleman; which few refreſhments, as ſhe termed them, ſeemed more calculated as a ſupply for an

Eaſt

East India voyage, than provision
for half a day's journey; but
that was the only way she had to
testify her regard. His departure was seen with pain by all.
Honest Tom Jenkins, however,
was most to be pitied. I believe
I have not mentioned that Tom,
from the time he had shewn so
much zeal in Harry's service, had
been a constant inmate in the family; shared with Harry in all
the advantages of bright example
and good education. Credit is
due to his parents, honest Jenkins and his wife, who had, from
his infancy, laid the best foundation

tion for good morals, TRUTH and
PIETY. Mr. Sinclair very foon
difcovered that he was totally
free from the mean tricks and low
arts, fo common in boys that are
not well taught. Tom poffeffed
an open, ingenuous temper, and
very foon, by the privilege of
being prefent at the hours of ftudy, with Harry and his uncle, became fuperior to his birth; indeed
what is birth but an empty found?
how many difgrace it, by unworthy conduct, and how often, for
want of fome foftering hand to
bring it forth, does humble merit
droop,

". And wafte its fragrance in the defart air."

Jenkins

Jenkins poffeffed fentiments and an integrity of foul, that would have done honour to the ·breaft of a duke. When the laft park gate clofed on his dear friends and benefactors, he burft into tears. " Alas !" faid he to him-felf, " what will become of me now ? who fhall. I have to fpeak to ? who will hear me read ? who will tell me when I do wrong, or applaud me if I am right ? Mrs. Steady is a very good wo-man, but her converfation is very different from that I hear in the parlour or the ftudy. But how wicked I am to be difcontented,

when

when I cannot be thankful enough for the bleſſings I enjoy. Was not Maſter Harry chearful and happy when he ſet out ? did he not ſmile, when he ſhook hands with me ? who is it then that I am grieving for ?—myſelf. Away ſelfiſh ſorrow ! God forgive me ! let me turn my thoughts to conſider how I can ſerve my maſter beſt, in his abſence. I will help the gardener to water his plants ; I will feed his birds, and I will comfort little Florio, who is as ſorrowful as a poor dog can be." Theſe reflections Tom made as he walked towards the houſe,

where

where he met Mrs. Steady coming to feek him. We are very partial to this good woman, but in ftrict truth we are obliged to confefs, that if fhe had a fault, it was being rather too loquacious ; and as talkers muft have hearers, fhe grew impatient for Tom's return, not being quite fo refined as to know the luxury of filent grief. "So, Mr. Jenkins, I wondered what was become of you. Dear me, thought I to myfelf, as fure as can be, they've popped him into the chariot, and taken him with them ;—then again, I thought, that could not be neither; for

what

what would they do with my
dear young gentleman, if he
'fhould be tired of riding; or, if
it fhould rain; but here you
ftand between hawk and buzzard,
fhilly fhally! Ah! you puts me
in mind of myfelf; juft fo I ufed
to ftand, mum chance, whenever
my papa and mamma went out
and left me at home."

The words " papa and mam-
ma," from the aged lips of the
corpulent Steady, had a fudden
effect on Tom's rifibility, and he
more than fmiled through his
tears, which had not yet ceafed
flowing. " Lord love you," con-

H   tinued

tinued fhe, " your very eyes is
fwelled out of your head. My
lady would never forgive me, if
fhe knew I let you take on fo;
almoſt the laſt words fhe faid to
me, was, " Take care of Tom."
Come, come into my room, and
let us chat a bit; though, to be
fure, I have feldom time to fpeak
a word. What with minding the
maids and the under-fervants,
and what with attending the fick
folks in the village and making
fhirts and fhifts for the Sunday
fcholars, linen for the poor little
innocent babies, and one thing
and another, I have no time for
nothing.

nothing. But come, fet with me
in my room; you will find
fomething to fay, if I cannot."

Tom knew how refpectable
Mrs. Steady was for her affection and integrity, and was fearful to offend her ; but he wifhed
to be permitted to fpend moft
of his time in Harry's ftudy,
who had not only given him
permiffion fo to do, but had
defired him to amufe and improve himfelf with his books.
However he indulged her the
firft day of the family's ab-
fence, as he knew her chief
                              difcourfe

difcourfe would be on the fubject moft pleafing to him, the merits of his benefactor.

CHAP.

CHAPTER V.

He that delicately bringeth up his servant
from a child, shall have him become his
son at length.—Proverbs, chap. xxix. ver. 25.

WE must now leave Tommy,
in this worthy housekeeper's
room, while we attend the tra-
vellers, who arrived after a short
and pleasant journey at Clairville Lodge, the magnificent seat
of Harry's father; too late, however,

ever, in the evening, for him to
be admitted into his brother's
room that night, or for his parents to make any obfervation
upon his manners and improvement. But when they had paffed the next day with him, his
polifhed manners, his elegant deportment, his fenfible and well-
bred anfwers to all their queftions,
ftruck them at once with admi-
ration and felf-condemnation;
they experienced the deepeft
mortification by the comparifon
they drew between him and his
rude awkward, ill-bred brother.
'What indeed can be fo fevere as
the

the feelings of a parent, if they
have any fenfe or judgment, at
finding, too late, their child def-
titute of thofe attainments which
lead to diftinction and efteem,
but if they were diftreffed at
only marking the difference in
the external manners of thefe two
boys, how would they have been
cut to the heart if they had
known Harry's intrinfic worth !
At prefent they had only time to
obferve the fair outfide of the
cafket, and knew not the ineftimable gem it contained within.

Harry, when permitted to attend in his brother's chamber,
addreffed

addreſſed him in gentle affectionate
terms of ſorrow for the cauſe of his
confinement. George's reception was coarſe and vulgar, and
ſuch as might be expected from a
boy of no education ; he could
not converſe, for he had no ideas;
at leaſt, not any that ſuited the
elegant turn of his brother's mind;
he could not diſcourſe of books,
for he had never read any ; he
had no memory, for it had never
been exerciſed ; a ſhort ſurly
no, or yes, compriſed the whole
of his converſation.

We cannot wonder that the
fortnight which Mr. Sinclair had
promiſed

promifed to pafs at his fifter's, dragged very heavily away; as the evenings were fpent in cards, and poor Harry left without any of his accuftomed amufements, or any companion that was at all congenial to him. He began to figh for home, and to wonder that Tom Jenkins had not, as he defired, written to him within a few mornings of their departure; however, the wifhed-for letter arrived, and was brought in while the family were at breakfaft, in George's chamber. Harry opened it with eagernefs, and his uncle defired him to read it out.

" What,

" What ! can Harry read writing ?" faid George. " I can but
juft read print hand, and have
not learnt to write yet." " I
fhould be very forry," faid Harry,
" if I could not both read letters, and write them ; I fhould
lofe the pleafure of correfpond-
ing with my friends ; and then,
to convince his brother, he began to read aloud the following
epiftle from honeft Tom.

Dear

Dear Mafter Harry,

Mrs. Steady fays I ought to begin *Honoured Sir,* but I think I like *Dear,* better, and you told me to write my thoughts. I heard your uncle fay, (and I mind every thing he fays) that a letter was worth nothing, that did not come from the heart; that fine people make fine fpeeches, that mean nothing; but that an honeft man fhould fcorn this. Now, if I was to fay, the houfe looked dull without you, and did not think fo, how mean I fhould be;

be; but it really does, and I am not the only one that wishes you back. Poor Florio looks quite sorrowful, and would not touch a bit of supper the day you went away. I have read a chapter in the Testament, every day, to Mrs. Steady, since you have been gone, and yesterday she got me to teach Nanny House's little girl, Watts's hymn about liars; for she broke a China cup, and then was so wicked as to say she did not do it, not considering

" That he who does one fault at first,
" And lies to hide it, makes it two."

Poor

Poor Nanny Houſe cried bit-
terly about it, as ſhe is afraid
your Aunt will not let her ſtay,
when ſhe knows it. For what
can be worſe than a liar ? Your
parrot called out yeſterday,
" Come back, come back." Mrs.
Steady thinks he has learnt it of
the Guinea fowls, but I think he
knows you are gone. The flowers you left in the ſtudy, are all
dead, and I think I ſhould be
dead too, if I was to ſit there
without you, the things all look
ſo diſmal. If they could ſpeak,
they would ſay how unhappy
they are. Mrs, Steady talks of
you

you all day long. She told me
she left one family, becaufe her
young mafter was fo mifchiev-
ous and rude, and the houfe was
like Bedlam ; but now she is
happy, and prays for your happinefs. She has been fadly fret-
ted thefe two days ; she has loft
the key of the medicine cheft.
Poor Geoffry has got the tooth-
ache, and she wanted to give him
fome phyfic for it; if he is not
better foon, she will get a new
lock put to it. The canary birds
that hang in the hall, never fing
now. What's very odd, James
Harris (the boy I bought the
bird's

bird's neft of,) has had one of
his eyes put out by an owl,
while he was looking for the
young ones. If he had minded
what you faid to him, Mafter
Harry, God Almighty would
have faved his eye. Parfon Roberts would not believe it, when
Mrs. Steady told him how you
fat in the tree, and what you
faid; fhe was very angry with
him, I never faw her in fuch a
rage. She told him, though he
was a very charming good man,
you had been brought up fo well,
that you was able to give as good
advice as he was; and to be fure

fhe

ſhe ſaid very true. So, Sir, pray
God ſend you home again.

I am your faithful Servant,

THOMAS JENKINS.

P. S. Mrs. Steady and all the
ſervants deſire their duty. The
poor dumb creatures look as if
they would ſay ſomething, if they
knew how.

"Pray, brother," ſaid Mrs.
Clairville, as ſoon as Harry had
finiſhed his letter, "Who is this
Tom Jenkins that makes ſo free
and writes ſuch ſtuff to Harry

the

the poor boy you have taken from charity into your fervice?"--"His conduct," replied Mr. Sinclair, "makes him a rich boy, and I hope Harry will always know the true diftinction between falfe and proper pride, and that he will choofe his friends and companions according to their character, and not according to their rank. When I advife him, as I do every one, to avoid low company, I mean low in mind. A prince, without proper education, may be vain, ignorant, felfifh, and unprincipled; a peafant, with good and early information, may pof-

I   lefs

fefs every virtue. Tom is an excellent boy, and will, I truft, reward me amply for my care of him, by giving Harry the bleffing of an attendant who will ferve him with fidelity and affection through life. I defire, Harry, you will anfwer his letter, and let us fee what you fay to him.; I think every line of his letter breathes ftrong regard for you, and he is, I am well affured, perfectly artlefs.

Harry waited only for this permiffion from his uncle, wifhing for nothing fo much as the pleafure of writing to Tom. He

obtained leave to go into his father's dressing-room, where he
was told he would find all ma-
terials for writing; but to his
great surprise, a servant, who was
in the room, prevented his going
in. "You shall not come here,
indeed, Sir."—" Why not," demanded Harry, " I have my father's leave to come here to
write."—" Ah, may be so ; my
master did not know, I am sure,
that all his things lay about. Besides, a fine thing indeed, your
coming here! here be fruit and
cakes, and all sorts of things in
his closet."—" What then," cried

Harry

Harry, blufhing with indigna-
tion.—" What then ! why I
knows well enough, what then.
You'll ftuff till you are fick, and
you'll ink the table all over, and
make the room I have juft been
cleaning, not fit to be feen, in a
fhort time, I'll warrant me. So
fay no more, for here you fha'n't
come. Has'n't my lady charged
me fifty times never to let Mafter
George into any of the beft a-
partments, and now he never
thinks of going into any of the
rooms, except the houfekeeper's
and the fervant's Hall.

Harry

Harry, though his temper was calm and unruffled on moſt occaſions, could not keep up his ſpirits, under this unjuſt and inſulting ſuſpicion, but burſt into tears. Mrs. Sinclair, paſſing near that part of the houſe at the time, heard him, and as ſhe well knew he never wept on trivial or frivolous occaſions, was much alarmed, and flew to know the cauſe of his diſtreſs ; which, when explained, hurt her as much as it had done Harry, and ſhe ſeverely repri-manded the ſervant, who, in excuſe for her offence, ſaid, that maſter George had ſo often done miſchief, mifchief, when he had been left in a room by himfelf, and then denied it, that fhe had been frequently brought into blame by him. " I am fure mafter George never comes no where, but what he's as rude as a bear." Mrs. Sinclair did not condefcend to explain to this woman the difference between the two brothers, efpecially as fhe found her abfurd enough to fuppofe all boys alike. She thought it more to the purpofe to chear and revive Harry's fpirits, whofe heart had been wounded to the quick, not fo much at the unworthy treatment offered to himfelf,

as

as at the fhocking character given
of his brother. If, indeed, as this
woman declared, he was a *liar*,
he muft be obliged to confider
him as the meaneft, and moft de-
fpicable being upon earth. To
be obliged to think thus of one
bound to him by the near and tender tie of brotherhood, cut him
to the foul ; and his aunt per-
ceiving he was in no fit mood for
writing, told him, upon confider-
ation, there would be no occafion
for it, as his uncle had fixed on
the next day for their departure.

This intelligence quickly re-
ftored Harry's chearfulnefs ; he

longed

longed to go back ; neither the amusements, the hours, or the society, of Clairville Lodge, suited his taste or genius : Harry was not the only one who thought of parting, with inward satisfaction. The Sinclairs sighed to return to their own house and neighbourhood, where they lived in elegant retirement.

The Clairvilles, especially Mrs. Clairville, were not sorry to lose the sight of those, whose conduct, particularly in their mode of bringing up a child, was so strong a reproach upon their own.

George was now sufficiently recovered

covered for his mother to pro-
pofe taking him to town, where
fhe languifhed to be herfelf; fo
that it required very little ceremony on the part of her brother
to take his leave. When the day
of departure came, Harry's little
poney feemed to partake in the
general fatisfaction, and to be fenfible, when his mafter mounted
him,' that his face was turned
towards home. He pranced,
neighed, frifked his long tail, and
a perfon lefs adroit than our hero,
would have found fome difficulty
in keeping his feat. The morning was uncommonly beautiful;

if

if a poet had been to defcribe it, he would have had a great deal to fay about Aurora, and Phœbus, and other great perfonages ; but it will beft fuit both our purpofe and our genius, to inform our readers, in plain words, that the fun fhone in fulleft luftre, on this amiable family. When they were within a few miles of their own houfe, a fervant was difpatched to announce their arrival: The do-meftics received the intelligence with unfeigned joy. Mrs. Steady buftled up ftairs, unfolded her beft muflin apron, and placed her-felf in the hall, to be ready with

her

her smiles and courtseys. · The parrot screamed—Florio wagged his tail—the canary birds made the hall resound with their song; but how shall I describe the sensations of Tommy Jenkins upon this occasion! He looked at himself to see if he was respectfully drest; he flew to wash his hands and comb his hair, though both hands and hair were in perfect order before; he ran to the gate to look if they were yet in sight, then back to Mrs. Steady, to ask if she saw the carriage out of the window; he began to think whether any thing was

lef-

left undone, that he had been bid
to do ; in short, Tom was not an
inftant ftill in mind or body. The
cottagers who faw the fervant
gallop up the avenue, begged to
know how long it would be before his honour and madam came;
and being told they were expected every minute, they got ready
to ring the bells at the adjoining
church.

Again I apply to my intelli-
gent readers to paint for me Harry's return, blufhing like a new
blown rofe at the bleffings he received as he paffed through the
village. Obferve how upright
he

he fits on his horfe, who curvets
and prances as if confcious of the
ineftimable burthen he had the
honour to bear. The bells ring-
ing, fervants flying, each wifhing
to be firft to receive him. Mrs.
Steady advancing, nodding, fmi_
ling, and courtfeying all the way
fhe went.—Tom Jenkins wild
with joy.—Such is the reception
of the benevolent man, who being good himfelf, makes all a-
round him glad and happy.

CHAP.

CHAPTER IV.

I have taught thee in the way of wisdom, I
have led thee in right paths.—Proverbs,
chap. iv. ver. 11.

IT was now the month of June,
the weather settled and serene,
the charming gardens of Sinclair
Castle were in their highest bloom
and beauty. The myrtle and
orange grove sent forth its strongest perfume; the carnation and

the

the rofe contended in adding fra.
grance to the month that gave
birth to Harry. It had been determined that his birth-day fhould
be celebrated with more than.
common fplendor, becaufe in a
fhort time after this aufpicious
day he was to leave home for
fchool. It was the cuftom of this
family to give an annual dinner
to the children of the Sunday
fchool, which was fupported
folely by the bounty of Mr.
Clairville. To cloathe the naked, feed the hungry, and inftruct
the ignorant, was the chief purpofe of this good man's life and
fortune;

fortune ; and we lament it is not
in our power to fay the fame of
every other man of fplendid property. This year, as Harry was
now of an age to enjoy the heart-
felt fatisfaction of feeing fo many
human creatures happy, and to
affift himfelf in planning the manner of the entertainment, it was
refolved that this feaft fhould
be held on his birth-day, and
that it fhould confequently be as
brilliant as poffible. Numerous
confultations were held with Mrs.
Steady, whofe bufinefs it was to
look to the baked meats. She
was ordered to prepare an am-

ple

ple quantity of pyes, puddings, plumb cakes, &c. in fhort, fuffi-cient fubflantial food for the fcholars, as well as to employ her fkill in the finer branches of cookery for the ornamental de-corations intended for the neigh-bouring gentry, who were invi-ted to a ball and fupper, which were to conclude the evening of this happy day. As it will not afford my readers any entertain-ment to be in the buftle of pre-paration, or to run backwards and forwards with Mr's. Steady, to enquire whether the foups fhall be all white or fome brown ; whe-

K   ther

ther the jellies shall stand at this
corner of the table, or the other,
whether the puddings for the
dinner shall be all plumb, or by
way of variety, some plain ; not
will it amuse them much more to
see Harry and Tom Jenkins se-
lecting and sorting the flowers
which Mrs. Sinclair, had ordered
to be hung in festoons round the
ball room and supper room. We
will then, suppose, if you please,
gentle readers, all things in the
best and highest stile possible,
ready prepared, and enter at once
upon the happy morn that gave
birth to the best of boys. The

sun

sun shone upon it, a finer sky was never seen. Harry, who arose with the lark, returned thanks to God for the blessings he was born to; and his friends at the same time offered their praises for the grace and goodness God had been pleased to bestow on him.

We have, I believe, mentioned before, that this family were accustomed to early rising, but on this day the whole house awoke with the day. The servants appeared in new liveries. Mrs. Steady, who had left nothing undone, put on a new silk

gown,

gown, which would, to ufe her own expreffion, fland alone. At nine o'clock the bells rang, and bands of mufic judicioufly difpo-fed in different parts of the houfe and gardens, began to perform chofen pieces of mufic, felected and adapted to the occafion, with infinite tafte, by Mrs. Sinclair. At eleven o'clock arrived the proceffion of children, preceded by a venerable pair, mafter and miftrefs of the fchool. There were twenty boys and as many girls, all in new and neat apparel. At the firft entrance of the ave-nue, the fervants were directed

to

to place on the breast of each, a
cockade of white ribbon, em-
broidered by Mrs. Sinclair, with
this emphatic motto, "Remember
thy Creator in the days of thy
youth." After they had passed
in procession, round the lawn,
they were conducted into the
great hall, where they were properly arranged ; the boys on one
side and the girls on the other.
The family attended, and by
Mr. Sinclair's desire, Mr. Roberts,
the clergyman of the parish, read
morning prayers, with a very excellent additional prayer, which
he had composed for the occasion.

sion. After prayers Mrs. Sinclair sung and played the 104th Psalm on a very fine organ, which stood in the hall, in which the children joined in heart and voice. The persons who taught them to know, to fear, to love their God, heard them thus join their voices to their Maker's praise, with inexpressible delight. Several times during the performance, both Harry and honest Tom were observed to wipe the tear of sensibility from their eyes. Upon the conclusion of this ceremony they were reconducted to the gardens, and at one o'clock, un-

der

der the shade of a double row of well-grown trees, they had two tables prepared for them, one for the girls, with the mistress at the head, and the other for the boys, where the master presided; a band of wind instruments played alternately at each table. Here they found a profusion of plain food; they had no occasion for the luxuries and incentives that depraved and indulged appetites require. Mrs. Steady, however, had dealt out the pies and plumb puddings with no sparing hand, well knowing the generosity of the donors.

To

. To a man of Mr. Sinclair's feelings, there could not be a more pleasing sight than this party of innocent children, trained by him *in the way they should go*, and now rewarded for their good behaviour, by his notice and indulgence.

To the glutton, the gamester, or the selfish man this would be a *dry* observation.

After dinner these young visitors were permitted to range the pleasure grounds, and to amuse themselves, each according to his fancy till evening, when benches were placed for them in the ball-
room,

room, that they might be still
further indulged with a sight of
the decorations and the company
that assembled in honour of the
day, At nine o'clock the ball
opened with a minuet by Harry
Clairville and Fanny Fairfax, an
elegant little girl about our hero's age ; she deserved the highest praise, but we cannot speak
higher of her than to say she was
worthy to be his partner. They
danced in a stile that made older
people blush, and very unwilling
to dance after them. Mrs. Sinclair was so much charmed with
this graceful, animated, little pair,
whom

whom she knew to be as amiable as they were beautiful, that
she was affected to tears, and wept
aloud to the surprife of all unfeeling fouls, or rather to the
wonder of thofe who had no
fouls at all. Soon after country
dances commenced, the Sunday
fcholars were permitted to retire,
each with a plumb cake and a
piece of filver. They departed,
each with a full refolution to be-
have well, as the only return
they could make their kind, indulgent benefactor, and indeed,
the only one he wifhed or defired.

" For bleffings ever wait on virtuous deeds,
" And, tho' a late, a fure reward fucceeds."

When

When the supper room was opened, which was early; for neither Harry nor Miss Fairfax were accustomed to sit up late, it exhibited a scene equally elegant and magnificent. Mrs. Steady had exerted all her skill, and with wonderful ingenuity had preserved the idea of the day. The splendid ornaments down the centre of the table, represented every species and every implement of industry; nor was the substantial forgot, (as we have seen at some tables) in the ornamental. There was

well

sufficient to satisfy the appetite, as
well as to gratify the taste of the
numerous guests who attended
this benevolent feast, which promoted chaste delight, nor left
regret behind.

" This place for social hours defign'd,
May care or anguish never find !
Come, every mufe, without reftraint,
Let genius prompt, and fancy paint ;
Let wit and mirth with friendly ftrife,
Chear the dull gloom, which faddens life ;
True wit, that firm to virtue's caufe,
Refpects religion and the laws ;
True mirth that chearfulnefs fupplies,
To modeft ears and decent eyes ;

Let

Let thefe indulge their livelieft fallies,
Both fcorn the canker'd help of malice
True to their country and their friend,
Both fcorn to flatter or offend."

CHAPTER VII.

Take fast hold of instruction, let her not go,
keep her, for she is thy life.—Proverbs,
chap. iv. ver. 13.

HARRY, who was now of an
age to require farther instruction,
and higher attainments than his
uncle was able to bestow, was in
a few days after his birth-day, to
quit home. In the choice of a tutor Mr. Clairville had not been

led

led, as many are, by fashion, or by the mean pride of placing his nephew where dukes and lords were to be his companions; he had been guided solely by the character of a man, who would, he was sure, pay as much attention to the moral as to the scholastic part of his pupil's character; who was, in the deep sense of the word, a gentleman, a scholar, and above all, a man of piety and strict morality.

When the morning of Harry's departure came, not a person in the house was to be seen without tears in their eyes. Our young hero,

hero, however, who had as much sensibility as any one, set them an example of firmness. He could not, indeed, quit such dear relations, who had watched over his infancy, with such tender, unremitting care, and who had studied to make every moment of his life honourable and happy, without severe pain at heart. But he knew that whatever they ordained, was intended for his benefit, and any unwillingness on his part, to comply with their wishes, would be improper, and highly distressing to them. He considered their feelings of more consequence fequence than his own, and he obeyed their commands with apparent chearfulnefs, and a ferenity of temper that proved his gratitude, his fenfe, and his regard for their peace. When the carriage came to the door, that was to convey him away, he flew into it, without daring to truft himfelf with that heart-rending word farewell ! nor did he hear the numerous voices that were raifed in prayers to God to blefs him. Tom Jenkins alone was filent ; for he was unable to fpeak. Mr. Sinclair, who accompanied him, gave him that praife

L   fo

so due to him, for his manly proper conduct, assured him the persons with whom he was going to place him, were such, as in all respects, he would be most happy with, and that they would take the best care of him, put him in mind, that the distance between them, was so short, that they should hear from each other often, and that there were three vacations in the year.

At parting, he presented him with a beautiful little watch, and the following lines with it, which Harry, as soon as he was settled, got by heart.

Little monitor, by thee
Let me learn what I should be
Learn the round of life to fill,
Uſeful and progreſſive ſtill,
Thou can'ſt gentle hints impart
How to regulate the heart.
When I wind thee up at night,
Mark each fault, and ſet thee right,
Let me ſearch my boſom too,
And my daily thoughts review;
Mark the movements of my mind,
Nor be eaſy, when I find
Latent errors riſe to yiew
Till all be regular and true.

As the diſtance to the private
ſeminary was only twenty miles
from Sinclair Caſtle, Mr. Sinclair
only ſtaid to introduce his dear
charge,

charge, and returned the same evening, knowing his lady would be impatient to hear how her dear Harry had supported his spirits. —She was much delighted with the account his uncle gave of his behaviour; all the comfort she knew in his absence, was in the society of Miss Fairfax. The lovely Fanny was the orphan daughter of a gentleman, nearly related to Mrs. Sinclair, who, since the death of her parents had adopted her entirely She was uncommonly clever sensible, and beautiful, and no one

knew

knew better how to improve her talents than Mrs. Sinclair, who now turned all her thoughts to her education.

CHAPTER VIII.

Poverty and shame shall be to him that refuseth instruction; but he that regardeth reproof shall be honoured.—Proverbs, chap. xiii.

ABOUT the same time that Harry was sent from home, Mr. and Mrs. Clairville sent George, with all his faults upon his head, to a public school. It is well if a boy, who has been carefully trained in the paths of virtue,

can

can pafs uncontaminated through the fiery ordeal of a public fchool; but to a boy like George, mife-rably prepared, they could not have given a finer finifh, or de-vifed a plan more fure to fix his habits of vice, folly, and extra-vagance. To prevail upon him however, to fet out, was no eafy tafk ; he poffeffed not the fine feelings and keen fenfibility of his amiable brother upon the fame occafion. No! all his mo-tions and actions were guided by the love he had for himfelf, and the pain of leaving his pa-rents occupied no part of his thoughts,

thoughts, when he stamped, roar-
ed, and declared he would not
stir. He considered only, that
he should probably have something to do, and that he should
not pass his time, quite so much
in ease and indolence as in the
stable or the servants-hall at
home. With a great deal of
persuasion, and an assurance
which was too true, that he
would have a great deal of time
to pass according to his own fancy; he at last, in a very ungracious
manner, consented to the day being fixed for his departure; he
was encouraged also, by his ill-

judging

judging mother, with a promise
of as much money as he wished,
a more grievous and destructive
indulgence than she had yet, in
her folly bestowed on him!

Thus prepared, and thus sent
forth, what can be expected to
follow, but increasing crimes
with increasing age, and that the
conduct, which in his childhood
could only be termed folly, would,
in his riper years become vice!
I will not disgust my readers by
following his steps through the
idle path he pursued in the course
of his scholastic life, or open to
their view scenes of riot and dis-

order;

order: nor will they be better p'eafed by attending him home at his vacation, where he was now admitted one of his mother's party in the drawing room. Shall we be enlightened, inſtruct-ed, or even amuſed, w th modern faſhionable converſation? Alas! no. We find it frivolous, abſurd, and too often improper, for the chaſte ear of youth.

Let us turn from this dark ſide, ar.d look towards the light which Harry diffuſes over our hiſtory, in whoſe breaſt every virtue was growing ſtronger, as well by the precept, as by the example

ample of his tutor, the worthy
Mr. Hampton. By diligence in
his studies, and decency and decorum in his whole conduct and
deportment, he endeared himfelf to every one. He never
omitted any duty enjoined him,
but performed every part of his
bufinefs with obedience and ala-
crity, and that not only from a
fenfe of advantage to himfelf,
but with a defire of fhewing his
gratitude and affection to him
who was labouring in his fervice.
He felt and knew the ufe and va-
lue of education, and how much
is due to thofe who take pains to

impart

impart and instil into us those
qualities which are necessary to
form the character of a scholar
and a Christian. Harry was totally free from any of those vile
tricks which often convert a boy
into a brute; he had too much
humanity to torment animals,
much less to tyrannize over boys
younger than himself. It cannot
be necessary to say that he ab-
horred an untruth, or that he
had a proper contempt for those
whom he found mean enough, at
any time, to shelter their faults
under the shallow artifice of eva-
sion; he excelled also in the

lighter

lighter and lefs material branches
of his education; he obeyed and
refpected all mafters; whatever
they undertook to teach, he con-
fidered it his duty to learn; he
danced elegantly. Nature, as if
determined to make him quite
perfect, had given him a melo-
dious voice and an admirable ear
for mufic; and he difcovered
infinite tafte and fkill in drawing. With application, joined
to abilities, and, at the fame time,
a ftrict obfervance of every religious and moral duty, who will
doubt, that a youth, under the
care of a pious, confcientious tutor,

tor, muſt become all that is good,
and all that is amiable. Such
every young man ought to be,
and ſuch every young man may
be, if parents neglect not their
part or duty, and are ſufficiently
attentive to the character of
thoſe to whom they give up the
taſk of inſtruction. But what
evil is there not to be looked for
from trifling and idle habits, in-
dolently allowed in childhood,
and too ſtrongly confirmed by
vicious example and bad company!

CHA>

CHAPTER IX.

Who can find a virtuous woman? for her price is far above rubies.—Proverbs, chap. xxxi, ver. 10.

SEVERAL years passed over the heads of these brothers; without any event worthy my reader's notice; the one regularly pursued the path that leads to happiness; the other still blindly followed

followed the way to deftruction.
Their different characters are
ftrongly marked in their ftyle of
writing. A reader, if he has any
tafte or delicacy, will be ftruck
with the natural elegance that
prevails in the ftyle of Harry,
and the vulgarity and grofs felfifhnefs that difcovers itfelf in
that of his brother. They are
not altered in a word from the
original. At the time of writing
them, Harry was fixteen, and
George feventeen.

Harry

Harry Clairville to his Aunt.

My dear Madam,

Time does not fly quite so fast here as it did at Sinclair Castle during the holidays; though I hope to make the hours appear less tedious between this and the next vacation, by industry. I thank you for the books I found in my trunk; but I thought, my dear madam, you understood better the usage of books here, than to have them so elegantly bound; they are better suited to the library of Miss M   Fairfax.

Fairfax. No boys make better
ufe, I believe, of the inside of
every author, than we do; but we
are very apt to disfigure, and
pay very little regard to the outfide. However, as your gift, I
will take all poffible care of
them. Pray tell Mifs Fairfax
that I will not fail to ftudy and
improve myfelf in Italian, that I
may be better able to converfe
with her, next time I return.
She did me the honour to defire
I would recommend fome books
to her; fhe is weary, fhe tells me,
of hiftory, which is an enumera-
tion only of crimes and follies;
but

but it is fit to know the evil with
which the world abounds, that
we may avoid it. Any recom-
mendation of books to one who
lives with you, dear madam,
would be prefumption in me ; for
all the knowledge I have is de-
rived from you. To your tafte,
to your judgement, then, I refer
her ; though I am not infenfible
to the compliment fhe has paid
me. I beg you will tell her, I
fhould be obliged to her for the
notes of that duet I attempted to
fing with her, that I may practice
it, and perform better the next
time I have the happinefs to be.

with

with you. I have no occasion
for money, and what you gave
me when I came away, was quite
sufficient. We have every thing
here we can wish. I must bid
you adieu! a few old Grecians
are waiting for me. Tell Miss
Fairfax, they are not such enter-
taining companions as Metastasio,
and some others we were talk-
ing of.

With affectionate compliments
to Miss Fairfax, and duty to my
uncle and yourself, I am,

My dear Madam,
Gratefully & affectionately yours,
HENRY CLAIRVILLE.
P.S. I send

P. S. I send you some lines enclosed, which, as they are my first essay in poetry, I beg may be seen by no one but yourself.

I.

I would not change my cheerful peace of mind,
   For all the wealth the world has to bestow;
The pure reflections of a heart refin'd,
   Yield the first bliss we can enjoy below.

II.

Hail, sovereign virtue! thou, whose mighty
     power
   Can blunt the sharpest grief affliction bears;
Can yield relief in misery's darkest hour,
   And raise the heart deprest by heaviest cares.

III.

Ah say, what pleasure can that bosom know
   Whose inmost folds the pangs of vice per—
     vades?

Each

Each flower the beast conceals a thorn belov
And i'e'en those they crown a moment fade.

IV.

As when on dreary Lybia's burning sand,
The cheerless traveller pursues his way,
Where pathless deserts, stretch'd on either hand,
Reflect with tenfold force the Solar ray,

V.

If chance the furious whirlwind sudden rise,
Mighty as Boreas, when he shakes the main,
Lifting huge clouds of sand into the skies,
Which threat'ning death, o'erhang the dark
en'd plain;

In vain, with fruitless search, and needless care,
He seeks from certain death a near retreat;
Worn by fatigue, and breathless with despair,
He waits in silent agony his fate.

A

A guilty confcience fills the mind with grief,
  And tinges every gaudy fcene with pain;

VIII.

Whilft virtue, though by penury depreft,
  Purfu'd by malice, perfidy, and ftrife,
Finds calm content in her own peaceful breaft,
  And rifes far above the ills of life.

George Clairville to his Mother.

Dear Mother,

      I got all your letters, but have had no time to anfwer none of them. I fhall be obliged to you to fend me fome new pocket-handkerchiefs, and fome new-fafhion waiftcoats, with three or four capes, of different co-
lours;

looked; and pray put to as much
money as you can into the par-
cel, for I am very poor. My father thought twenty guineas was
a great deal to bring to school;
but it is not half so much as Lord
Squander and Sir Harry Harpy
bring with them. Breakfasting
at the coffee house, as we do,
costs a good deal, and you don't
like I should be in debt. Tell
the butler he is very clear sighted
with his old eyes, but it was not
me he saw at Ascot races, it was
another boy very like me. I
have lost the watch you gave me;
you had better send me another,

and

and fay nothing of it to my father,
I have hurt my thumb in a bat-
tle with Lord Squander, who
bragged of having more money
than you could afford to give
him, fo you muft excufe the bad
writing. Send the things directly,
and don't forget the money. I
don't think there is any occafion
to learn French, or dancing; the
dancing mafter is fuch a queer
fellow, we always quiz him.

    I am

     Your dutiful Son,

     GEORGE CLAIRVILLE.

We

We fhall make no comment on thefe letters; it requires very little difcernment to mark the contraft of character, fo ftrongly delineated.

Mrs. Sinclair had employed her whole time in embellifhing with every brilliant accomplifh_ ment, the natural elegant mind of her favourite Fanny. We wifh to prefent a picture of her to our readers, at the age of fif- teen; but where fhall we find lan- guage to do juflice to a form, pof- fefling every grace and beauty, and a mind replete with every virtue? Her countenance, the
true

true emblem of her heart, evi-
dently displayed the mildness and
serenity of her temper. Truth,
honour, integrity, piety, delicacy,
purity, in a word every solid virtue was implanted in her soul ;
and highly adorned with every
ornamental part of education,
she excelled in dancing, drawing,
music, &c. She had acquired a
sufficient taste for the real beauties
of literature to deter her from
perusing the trash that is so libe-
rally bestowed on the public, under the name of novels ; if any
such had fallen in her way, she
dreamed not of knights in ar-
mour

mour; she had no fancied female friend to scribble to, nor
had she ever heard of heroines,
who, urged on by "the thorny
point of bare distress," embroider
in garrets to support themselves.
It will be needless to add, that she
was totally free from that great
deformer of the female character,
affectation; her modest diffidence
often kept her silent, in a circle
of loquacious females, where, if
sense and information had been
considered as necessary ingre-
dients in conversation, she would
have been the only speaker. She
could converse without having
recourse

recourse to such topics as fashionable places of amusement, dress, or the more pernicious and disgusting subject of flirts and beaux. *Scandal*, base talk! fell not from her lips, nor indeed ever came to her ears; the sense and judgment of Mrs. Sinclair made her nice in the choice of her company, especially while she had such dear persons under her care, who, on account of their youth, were open to every impression.

We do not wonder that the lovely Fanny was the delight and comfort of her life; she endeared

deared

deared herself by her condefcen-
fion, her obedience, her affectionate and attentive difpofition, and
her turn for the domeftic enjoy-
ments of life. She could be
happy without feeking for amufement in affemblies, cards, &c.
In a word, fhe was what every
young woman ought to be, and
prefents us another inftance of
the happy effects that never fail
to reward early and unremitting
care and attention.

CHAPTER X.

Frowardness is in his heart, he defireth mifchief continually, he foweth difcord.—Proverbs, chap. vi. ver. 14.

EACH returning vacation that brought Harry home, was anxioufly expected at Sinclair Caftle; he added to the brilliancy of their fociety, and converfation gladdened every hour and cheered every heart. At one of thefe periods,

periods, upon the day on which
he was to arrive, to their great
furprize, fome hours before him,
George Clairville made his appearance ; he had very feldom
vifited his uncle, never without
invitation, and his conduct had
given fufficient occafion for that
invitation to have ceafed for fome
time ; they now felt therefore,
how much his prefence would
take from the pleafure they had
propofed to themfelves during
his brother's ftay with them ; po-
litenefs, however, forced them to
conceal their chagrin, but with
what mingled pity and contempt,
did

did they behold him, when by a letter from his father, the cause of his visit was explained. His father entreated Mr. Sinclair to receive him, as he was obliged to attend Mrs. Clairville to Lisbon, on account of the dangerous state of health to which her son's conduct had reduced her, and as it would be only a few weeks before he was to go to the university, hoped, for that interval, they would, in pity to her, protect him. Mr. Sinclair beheld his nephew with more disgust than ever, after he had read this letter, but respect to his sister's request, added to

N his

his natural good breeding and
hofpitality, made him diffemble
his feelings ; and with the beft
grace he could, he bid George
welcome to his houfe, where he
had not been long, before the
gloom which he had occafioned
was difpelled by Harry's arrival.
The filent folemnity that reigned
in the houfe a minute before, was
changed to a tumult of joy. Mrs
Sinclair and Mifs Fairfax laid
afide their work ; Mr. Sinclair's
countenance brightened again ;
honeft Tom came blufhing in, to
afk his friend and mafter how he
did ; the old butler and Mrs.
Steady

Steady joftled each other at the door, ftriving which fhould get in firft to make the fame enquiry; Mrs. Steady very fhrewdly obferved there was no need to afk Mr. Harry how he did, he looked fo charming. Her mafter fmiled —Mifs Fairfax blufhed. Why Mifs Fairfax blufhed we cannot exactly fay, probably at finding her thoughts agree with an old houfekeeper's. George, who did not want natural underftanding, though it was loft in idlenefs and neglect, could not but perceive the different reception given to him and to his brother, and determined

termined in his heart to take re-
venge. To do him juftice, however, it was more to indulge a ha-
bit of wanton fport, than from
any malice, that he formed this
refolution. Harry's happinefs
was for fome time confiderably
broken in upon by the news of
his mother's illnefs; for though
he had not lived much with them,
nor ever received from them any
ftrong marks of regard, he had
a great natural affection for his
parents; a principle which Mr.
Sinclair took care to inculcate
and nourifh in him. Accounts
however having been received of
Mrs.

Mrs. Clairville's being rather better, and the higheſt hopes being
entertained from her voyage to
Liſbon, the family at Sinclair
Caſtle gave way freely to all the
mirth and joy that Harry's company naturally diffuſed, and not
even George's preſence could
diſpel. Reading, working, walking, or riding, alternately employed the morning ; in muſic, ſing-
ing, or dancing, gaily paſſed the
evening. All was love and harmony, except in the mind of
George, who envied happineſs he
had not taſte to enjoy. He hated
muſic, becauſe he did not under-
ſtand

ftand it; for the fame reafon he
difliked dancing, becaufe he had
not learnt to excel in it. Books
were his averfion for they told
him truths he could not bear to
hear. In the midft of the fineft
piece of mufic, he generally left
the room, and would prefer feeing
the groom rub down the horfes
to hearing Mifs Fairfax play or
fing, though fhe did both in the
higheft ftile. At other times he
found amufement in frightening
poor Steady and the maids by
throwing fquibs and crackers
amongft them. One evening
with more ill humour than wit, he

went

went into the room where a defert was fet out with more than common care, for an entertainment the next day, and overturned the whole ; difplaced and jumbled all things together, put vinegar to the creams, pepper and falt to the ices, and muftard and oil to the preferves. Fortunately for poor Mrs. Steady fhe found out the mifchief in time to prepare again for the table, or it would have been the old lady's death. As it was, fhe declared, if Mr. George was to ftay there much longer, dear as fhe loved her lady, fhe muft go away. " He

does

does not," said she, " know what to do with himself, so he is always in mischief."—A very shrewd observation of Mrs. Steady's, for there is nothing which leads more certainly to crimes and follies than not knowing how to pass our vacant hours ; and you might as well let a bear loose about your house, as an uneducated ignorant boy. They were sitting one evening, a family party, all however employed in some way or other, but George, who was fast asleep, when the butler came i with the parrot's cage empty in his hand. " Oh ! Mr. Harry," said

he, "fomebody has been wicked
enough to let poor Poll out; nobody has been in the room fince
fhe was fed, they all declare, but
Mr. George; fure he would never do fuch a cruel thing, though,
(I beg your pardon, Sir,) I do
think he is bad enough, and
what's worfe, (but I thought it
proper to tell you, Sir,) Tom Jenkins has been gone feveral hours,
nobody knows where; its pitch
dark, and rains as hard as it can
pour. As foon as he heard the
poor bird was gone, he faid he
knew how much you loved it, and
that you had taught it to call Mifs
Fanny,

Fanny, and vowed he would not come back till he had found it; for my part I don't know which to be moſt ſorry for, poor Poll, or Tom; I greatly fear he will come to ſome harm, for he is not uſed to be out in the night." Mr. Sinclair awoke his nephew George, with no gentle touch, and demanded in a ſtern accent, " did you, ſir, let looſe the bird which you knew your brother valued ?" George rubbed his eyes, and muttered out, " Hang the Parrot, I did not know any thing about its being a favourite; it made a horrid noiſe, ſo I put it

up

up in a tree, and I fhould have fetched it in again if I had not forgot it; but its very foolifh to be fo fond of birds, and make fuch a fufs about them." " I wifh, Sir," faid his uncle, " you were fond of things as innocent." What more he might have faid on the occafion was prevented by Tom's coming in, dripping wet, and Poll chattering and biting his fingers all the way he came. " Oh, my good friend Tom," faid Harry, " I am glad to fee you; where did you find my poor parrot?" "Why, Sir," replied Tom, " I was direct-ed by fome boys, who faw her fly

towards

towards Farmer Cartwright's, and after going some way I began to despair, as it grew dark, of ever finding her, when fortunately I knocked at the door of a cottage to beg shelter from the rain, which then fell in torrents. I was answered by an old woman, who cried out, " Ah! stop a little ; I would not let you in if you were a king, till I have killed this devil. You toad you, do you think you shall spoil my garden and bite my fingers for nothing? I'll roast you for supper, that I will. Ah! you may fly, I'll fetch you down, I warrant me." If it had not been

for

for the word fly, and Poll being
uppermoft in my imagination, I
believe I fhould have flown myfelf, at the found of intended mur-
der, in fuch a lonely place, and in
fuch a difmal night; but convinced
in my own mind, that her enemy
was no other than your parrot,
Sir, and thinking there was no
time to be loft, I put my foot to
the door, which I found it required no great force to burft open,
when I beheld, as I had fufpected,
poor Poll feated upon a cup-
board's head, and defending her—
felf very fkilfully againt the old
woman and her broom; the mo-

ment

ment I appeared, the bird called
out, as I had taught her, "How
do you do, Tom." Upon hearing so clear a sentence, so aptly
applied from the voice of a bird,
the old woman fell into an agony
of surprise and horror, and knelt
first to Poll and then to me, be-
seeching us not to kill her; for
she concluded one to be a witch
and the other a wizard; and it
was with no small difficulty, I
convinced her that we intended
her no harm. Finding that Mrs.
Poll had made great depredation
on her garden and her fingers, I
repaid the damage as well as I was

able,

able, and supplied her with the
means of procuring a better supper, than if, as she designed, she
had killed and roasted our poor
bird here. We parted good
friends, and to her lanthorn I am
indebted for finding my way
home."

This story of Tom's, restored
peace and good humour again to
all. George, at Harry's request,
was forgiven. Mrs. Poll was
caressed and fed ; and her kind
defender, Tom, amply rewarded
for his trouble, by the thanks and
praises of a master who was dearer
to him than his life. Mr. Sinclair,

who

who faw much malice in this act
of George's, determined to haften
his departure, in which refolution
he was confirmed by a circum-
ftance which happened foon after Poll's adventure. We mention
indeed, only a few of the many
tranfactions of this idle youth,
which rendered his abode uneafy
to this regular and delightful family. To tell all his exploits
would difguft and tire. Jenkins
came in one morning during
breakfaft, with a meffage from a
farmer in the neighbourhood, who
defired to return two guineas to
Mr..Harry Clairville. He was
very

very angry with his wife when he
came home, for taking more than
three out of the five he had been
fo good as to fend. Harry,
deeply blufhing, with much hefi-
tation and impatience in his manner, exclaimed, " No! no! no! tell
him to take the whole; it is not
too much; but why did you bring
it here ? Foolifh man! why did
he or you fay any thing about it?"
" Nay," faid Mr. and Mrs. Sinclair both in a breath, " now, my
dear Harry, you have raifed a curiofity that muft be fatisfied."

Mifs Fairfax, who had rifen from
breakfaft, to finifh a painting which

O   fhe

fhe was about, made the leaves
blue and the flowers green, and
George now thought it his turn
to triumph. " Oh! oh!" faid he,
" the demure, the peerlefs Harry,
¹s not without his fchemes, his fe-
crets, and his private expences.
Pray tell us Harry, what makes
you blufh fo?" Nothing but a fneer
like this, would have provoked
him to fay, "You, brother! it is
for you I blufh!" More than this,
not all his aunt's perfuafion, his
uncle's commands, or the lovely
Fanny's inquifitive looks, would
force from him. But Tom Jenkins, not quite fo refined as his
                                    mafter,

mafter, at leaft infenfible to every
fenfation but that of refentment,
for the fufpicion caft on Harry's
honour, with fome warmth declared, heedlefs of Harry's nods
and figns to keep him filent, that
the money was fent to the Farmer, to make him amends for the
damage Mr. George had done to
his corn, and the injury done to
his man, by beating him, for en-
deavouring to prevent his riding
over it. " I was fent, Sir," faid he to
Mr. Sinclair, " for fear the knowledge of it fhould give you any
uneafinefs."—" I thought indeed,"
faid Mr. Sinclair,—" I thought !"
                    interrupted

interrupted his aunt, and " I
thought!" fell like gentle echo
from the lips of Fanny, and like
echo might have died away, if
Harry had not turned round, and
in the fofteft accents, demanded
" What did my fweeteft Fanny
condefcend to think?" Whether
the dear maid could anfwer this,
or whether fhe would have dif-
clofed her thoughts to him, innocent as they were, remains a doubt;
for George, in courfe and loud
language, accompanied by a fneer,
anfwered for her, " think! why
fhe thinks you all perfection I
fuppofe."—" Nephew Clairville,"
said

faid Mr. Sinclair, with a more
ftern countenance than we thought
him able to put on, " retire to
your dreffing room ; deep refentment, like deep grief, is dumb.
The time is now come for your
departure ; my carriage fhall be
ready in half an hour, to convey
you to the univerfity. Remember when you are there, that your
mother's life or death is in your
power. If fuch a conviction has
no influence on your conduct, all
I can fay will have no avail. If
I hear that you live a regular,
proper life, with due attention to
your ftudies, I will recieve you
again,

again, and all that has paſt ſhall be forgotten."

His aunt and Harry felt more for him on this humiliating occaſion, much more, it muſt be confeſſed, than he felt for himſelf. Even Fanny, in her compaſſion, pardoned his having encreaſed the roſes on her cheeks. The miſguided youth, unfeeling as he was unprincipled, quitted theſe amiable relations without regret, and without mortification at knowing he was not regretted. His departure reſtored the caſtle to its wonted charm of peace and order. Harry could read, ſing, or

walk

walk with Fanny, free from
coarfe jokes, or noify interrup-
tions. Fanny could enjoy the
company of her tame birds and
animals, without fear of their being tormented or deftroyed.
Tom Jenkins rejoiced, for the
fake of the dogs and horfes. Mrs.
Steady prayed God to forgive her,
but fhe wifhed fhe might never
fee his face again. Phrophetic
wifh! when George left his uncle's, he left it for ever.

CHAPTER XI.

As righteoufnefs tendeth unto life, fo he that
purfueth evil, purfueth it to his own death.—
Proverbs, chap. xvii. ver. 17.

TOO faft fly the moments that
bring on the day of fepara-
tion from thofe we love; and
time, who drags a heavy chain
amidft the worthlefs and the idle,
with the virtuous, and, of courfe,
the happy, fleets imperceptibly
away. It had been determined
that

that Harry fhould follow his brother to the univerfity in fix months; alas! the moment came, when they thought a very few weeks had paffed. His ftay, however, was for fome time prolonged, from a fatal caufe. A letter from his father informed him, that his mother had died of a broken heart, that he himfelf had determined to end his days in a foreign country, his own being rendered miferable to him by the lofs of his wife, and the conduct of his eldeft fon, who was equally loft to him, to the world, and to himfelf; that he had in

vain,

vain, tried every art to reclaim him, but he neither regarded his advice, nor anfwered his letters ; and that he was well informed, his mother's unhappy death had made no impreffion on, or alter-ation in him. That he had taken care to make a provifion for him, fufficient for the neceffaries of life, and after referving enough for the purpofes of retirement, had made over his whole eftate to Harry. This information, to a fordid man, might have been a confolation, but he had not been trained in the fchool of felfifhnefs; and the latter part of the letter, pained

pained him equally with the reft.
But in the fame moment that he
recieved the intelligence, he refolved, (though his father had taken proper care that he fhould
not refign the eftate,) that his
brother fhould enjoy the profits
of it. It was not to be expected,
eftranged as he had been from
his parents, from his earlieft infancy, that he fhould feel for
them the ftrong affection which
was due to his uncle and aunt;
yet he poffeffed a fenfibility of
heart, that made him fuffer the
fevereft forrow for the misfor-
tunes of his family ; and it was a
long

long time after this grievous account, before he had health or
spirits to quit his friends, or en-
counter a meeting with his brother. It was a comfort to him
that he was not to be of the same
college; for, as if unworthy bo-
dies had the power of attracting
each other, George was placed
where slender discipline and bad
society encreased his failings, and
added to them the destructive vice
of drinking. Harry was sent to
a college of a very different cast,
the head of it was a man of a
very superior nature; in him
were united every quality that
can

can enrich the foul, and all the polifhed elegance that can adorn the man. No wonder that the fociety under fuch a mafter, fhould be fuperior to any other in the univerfity, and there our hero found himfelf as happy as he could be any where from home. He had a tutor, almoft as young as himfelf, whom we would attempt to praife, if new words could be coined for the purpofe, but language fails ; the common epithets, to common merit, will not convey an adequate idea of his worth ; and we muft imitate the painter, who draws a curtain,

to

to conceal the feelings he found his art unable to exprefs.

Harry feldom faw his brother, as George carefully avoided the fociety of one fo uncongenial to himfelf ; but poor Harry was often deeply mortified to find that in every drunken riot in the ftreet, or what too often difgraces the univerfity, noify tumults at public places, George Clairville was always at the head. This uneafinefs, however, was of fhort duration ; as every crime brings its own punifhment, George, by his folly and intemperance, foon put an end to his wretched life. In

the

the firſt half year of Harry's re-
ſidence at Oxford, and in a
twelvemonth after the death of
his mother, at a midnight revel,
where he had boaſted that he
could drink even more than his
companions, he was ſeized with a
fever, and in three days, without
one hope to ſooth the bed of death,
or one friend to ſhed for him a
pitying tear, he died.

Mr. Sinclair, as ſoon as he
heared the melancholy news, haſt-
ened to bring his nephew home,
knowing that was the place moſt
likely to ſooth his ſorrow, and re-
cruit his ſtrength : He could not
be

be fuppofed to regret his brother,
as one who had endeared himfelf
by virtuous deeds and friendly in-
tercourfe; the forrow for fuch a
youth as George, muft be tran-
fitory, for he was dead to his family, even while he lived, and
they had only to regret, that
longer time was not allowed him
for repentance.

In a few months, Harry returned to college, where his uncle
wifhed him to remain fomewhat
longer, in a fociety fo honourable,
to encreafe the number of his
friends, and enlarge the circle of
his acquaintance. To improve
him

him, it was needlefs; he was a
brilliant fcholar, and in the fulleft and beft fenfe of the word, a
gentleman, of ftrict integrity and
polifhed manners; in a word, he
was a good Chriftian. Adored
by his relations, refpected by his
domeftics, and truly valued by
his friends, at the age of twenty-
one, he took poffeffion of a fplendid eftate. After this, his firft
care was to feek the retreat of his
father, whom he fucceeded in
perfuading to return to England
with him, and had the fatisfaction
to fmooth, and foften the re-
mainder of a life, endangered by
the

the profligacy of his brother.
On his return, he was bleft with
the hand of the beautiful and
amiable Mifs Fairfax; that he
had long poffeffed her heart will
be gueffed ; indeed the ftrongeft
affection, founded on mutual
efteem, had long fubfifted between
them.

" What is the world to fuch,
Its pomp, its pleafures, and its nonfenfe all !
Who in each other clafp whatever fair
High fancy forms, and lavifh hearts can wifh ;
Something than beauty dearer, fhould they look
Or on the mind, or mind illumin'd face ;
Truth, goodnefs, honour, harmony, and love,
The richeft bounty of approving heaven."

THE END.